ROALD DAHL

THE BFG's GLORIUMPTIOUS JOURNAL

illustrated by Quentin Blake

Grosset & Dunlap
An Imprint of Penguin Random House

GROSSET & DUNLAP

Penguin Young Readers Group
An Imprint of Penguin Random House LLC

Additional text by Allison Fabian

Frobscottle recipe originally published in *Roald Dahl's Revolting Recipes*.

Text copyright © 2016 by Roald Dahl Nominee Ltd. Illustrations copyright © 1982 by Quentin Blake. All rights reserved. Published in 2016 by Grosset & Dunlap, an imprint of Penguin Random House LLC, 345 Hudson Street, New York, New York 10014. GROSSET & DUNLAP is a trademark of Penguin Random House LLC. Manufactured in China.

ISBN 978-1-101-99598-3   10 9 8 7 6 5 4 3 2 1

Given to
Westan
6 July 2016
by
Grandma
Alice Guerra

The witching hour, somebody once whispered to Sophie, was a special moment in the middle of the night when every child and every grown-up was in a deep deep sleep, and all the dark things came out from hiding and had the world to themselves.

Would you take a walk outside during the witching hour? What would you take with you?

What sorts of creatures do you think are about at the witching hour? What are they doing?

_____

_____

_____

_____

_____

Draw a picture of the wildest, most frightening thing you've seen during the witching hour.

The next moment, a huge hand with pale fingers came snaking in through the window. This was followed by an arm, an arm as thick as a tree-trunk, and the arm, the hand, the fingers were reaching out across the room toward Sophie's bed.

This time Sophie really did scream, but only for a second because very quickly the huge hand clamped down over her blanket and the scream was smothered by the bedclothes.

What would you do if you saw a giant reaching into your bedroom like Sophie did? Would you be afraid? Would you tell someone?

What's the scariest thing that's ever happened to you?

_____

_____

_____

_____

_____

_____

_____

_____

_____

_____

_____

_____

_____

What do you do when you get scared?

_____

_____

_____

_____

_____

_____

_____

_____

Who can you talk to about how you feel?

_____

_____

_____

_____

_____

_____

What helps make you feel brave when you are nervous?

_____

_____

_____

_____

_____

_____

_____

_____

_____

_____

_____

_____

_____

Out of the village he ran, and soon they were racing across the moonlit fields. The hedges dividing the fields were no problem to the Giant. He simply strode over them. A wide river appeared in his path. He crossed it in one flying stride.

The Giant is moving awfully fast. What would you do if you could run that fast? Where would you go, and who would you take?

THE BFG

"I is hungry!" the Giant boomed. He grinned, showing massive square teeth. The teeth were very white and very square and they sat in his mouth like huge slices of white bread.

"P . . . please don't eat me," Sophie stammered.

The Giant let out a bellow of laughter.

What would you say to a giant if it wanted to eat you? Do you think you could convince it to leave you alone?

NEW FRIENDS

"Me!" shouted the Giant, his mighty voice making the glass jars rattle on their shelves. "Me gobbling up human beans! This I never! The others, yes! All the others is gobbling them up every night, but not me! I is a freaky Giant! I is a nice and jumbly Giant! I is the only nice and jumbly Giant in Giant Country! I is the BIG FRIENDLY GIANT! I is the BFG. What is your name?"

What would it be like to meet a Big Friendly Giant?

_____

_____

_____

_____

_____

_____

**Do you like meeting new people?
Or do you feel shy?**

_____

_____

_____

_____

_____

**What are some tips you would give a shy
person when they meet somebody new?**

_____

_____

_____

_____

_____

_____

_____

_____

Help the BFG get to know you better by telling him about some of your FAVORITE things:

FAVORITE COLOR:

FAVORITE MOVIE:

FAVORITE FOOD:

FAVORITE SINGER:

FAVORITE ANIMAL:

FAVORITE HOLIDAY:

FAVORITE BOOK:

The BFG is very sad when Sophie tells him about her life at home. If she broke a rule, she would be locked in the dark cellar without any food or drink!

What happens if you
break a rule?

_____

_____

_____

_____

What are some of the rules you
have to follow at school or home?

_____

_____

_____

_____

_____

_____

The BFG lives in a big cave with a huge table and chair, and lots of jars on every shelf.

If you lived in a cave, what would it look like? Where would you put all your favorite things? Draw a picture of your cave here!

The BFG has such sensitive ears that he can hear all the secret whisperings of the world. He can hear the music of the stars, the screaming of flowers being picked, and the little ants chittering to each other in the soil.

If you had special ears like the BFG, what would you most like to hear?

_____

_____

_____

_____

_____

_____

_____

_____

_____

_____

_____

_____

SPIDER SONGS

"Spiders is also talking a great deal. You might not be thinking it but spiders is the most tremendous natterboxes. And when they is spinning their webs, they is singing all the time. They is singing sweeter than a nightingull."

Write a song for a spider spinning a new web.
What do you think it is singing about?

_____

_____

_____

_____

_____

_____

_____

SNOZZCUMBERS

Because the BFG doesn't eat human beans like other giants, he has to eat a disgusting vegetable called the SNOZZCUMBER.

Do you like eating vegetables? Which ones do you like, and which ones taste nasty?

LIKE   ## NASTY

_____   _____

_____   _____

_____   _____

_____   _____

_____   _____

_____   _____

_____   _____

_____   _____

_____   _____

FROBSCOTTLE!

The BFG wants to share his **DELUMPTUOUS** fizzy **FROBSCOTTLE** with you and Sophie! Here's how to make your own:

YOU WILL NEED:

Blender

Sieve

8 kiwi fruits, peeled

Juice of **1½** limes

4 ounces raspberry drinking yogurt

8 ounces lemonade

12 ounces cream soda

NOTE: If you wish to use ordinary yogurt instead of drinking yogurt, add it in step 1 and puree it along with the kiwis and lime juice.

INSTRUCTIONS:

1. Place the kiwis and lime juice in a blender or food processor and puree until liquefied.

2. Push the mixture through a sieve. (A few seeds will escape, but this doesn't matter.)

3. Add the drinking yogurt and mix.

4. Gradually mix in the lemonade.

5. Pour in the cream soda, mix, and serve.

WHIZZPOPPERS!

With FROBSCOTTLE comes WHIZZPOPPERS!

The BFG loves **WHIZZPOPPER** stories! Do you have a funny or embarrassing **WHIZZPOPPING** story?

_____

_____

_____

_____

_____

_____

_____

_____

_____

_____

GIANT COUNTRY

"We is in Giant Country now! Giants is everywhere around! Out there us has the famous Bonecrunching Giant! Bonecrunching Giant crunches up two whoppsy-whiffling human beans for supper every night!"

The BFG is going to take you on a tour of Giant Country. You'll get to see all the animals that only live there, like the HUMPLECRIMPS, WRAPRASCALS, and CRUMPSCODDLES.

Draw pictures of your favorite Giant Country animals, and describe the sounds they make!

"The matter with human beans," the BFG went on, "is that they is absolutely refusing to believe in anything unless they is actually seeing it right in front of their own schnozzles. Of course quogwinkles is existing. I is meeting them oftenly. I is even chittering to them."

Do you believe in things that you've never seen in real life? Why or why not? What are some things you believe in that you've never actually seen?

Do you think Sophie changed her mind about believing in the **QUOGWINKLES** after spending more time with the BFG? Why or why not?

WHERE DO GIANTS COME FROM?

"Giants *appears* and that's all there is to it. They simply *appears*, the same way as the sun and the stars."

If five brand-new giants suddenly appeared, what would their horrid names be?

1. _____   4. _____

2. _____   5. _____

3. _____

Draw a picture of the most FOULSOME, SQUIFFLEROTTER giant of them all!

What would your name be if you were a giant? Pick your favorite food or a silly word and then add —EATER, —MUNCHER, —MASHER, or —CRUNCHER to the end.

Then draw yourself as a giant!

Giants sleep only two to three hours each night! If you needed to sleep only three hours, you'd have lots of extra time. What would you do with all that time?

Each giant has his own special way of catching and eating human beans. The Meatdripper likes to pretend he is a tree in the park so he can snatch people having picnics. Gizzardgulper prefers to hide on top of city buildings and choose from all the people walking on the street, like a menu.

How do you think these giants like to catch their dinner?

MANHUGGER

BLOODBOTTLER

_____

_____

_____

_____

THE BUTCHER BOY

BONECRUNCHER

DREAM CATCHING

"Dreams," he said, "is very mysterious things. They is floating around in the air like little wispy-misty bubbles. And all the time they is searching for sleeping people."

"How do you catch them?"

"The same way you is catching butteryflies," the BFG answered. "With a net."

A good catcher of dreams moves quietly and catches dreams gently. Draw a design for the best dream-catching net you can imagine. Maybe the BFG will help you build it!

35

DREAM COUNTRY

Every minute, the mist became thicker. The air became colder still and everything became paler and paler until soon there was nothing but gray and white all around them. They were in a country of swirling mists and ghostly vapors. There was some sort of grass underfoot but it was not green. It was ashy gray.

Imagine that you are visiting Dream Country. What does it smell like? What does the air feel like? Do you feel afraid, excited, or something else?

Draw a picture of you with Sophie and the BFG in Dream Country.

DREAM MUSIC

"A dream," he said, "as it goes whiffling through the night air, is making a tiny little buzzing-humming noise. But this little buzzy-hum is so silvery soft, it is impossible for a human bean to be hearing it."

What do you think dreams sound like? What kind of message are they sending? Does it come in words, or is it a feeling?

What's your favorite kind of music? Do you have a favorite song to sing?

_____

_____

_____

_____

_____

What do you think your dreams sound like?

_____

_____

_____

_____

_____

_____

_____

GOLDEN PHIZZWIZARDS!

Sophie and the BFG caught
four golden PHIZZWIZARD dreams!
Help them label the new
dreams.

I AM SWIMMING DEEP IN THE OCEAN...

_____

_____

_____

_____

I AM WALKING INTO A LARGE CASTLE...

_____

_____

_____

_____

_____

THERE IS A WIZARD AT MY HOUSE ASKING ME TO HELP HIM...

_____

_____

_____

_____

_____

_____

_____

EVERYONE AT SCHOOL WILL BE SO IMPRESSED BECAUSE...

_____

_____

_____

_____

_____

_____

_____

To whom would you give your four golden PHIZZWIZARDS, if you could? Don't accidentally blow any TROGGLEHUMPERS through their windows! (Trogglehumpers are the very worst dreams!)

Who should dream the swimming dream? Why?

_____

_____

_____

_____

The wizard dream?

_____

_____

_____

_____

How about the dream in the large castle?

_____

_____

_____

_____

Who will get the dream that takes place in school?

_____

_____

_____

_____

What's the best WINKSQUIFFLER good dream
you've ever had? Write the whole story here
so you don't forget it!

DREAM JOURNAL

Do you ever have strange or exciting dreams? Keep a dream journal for a week so you can remember them. If you don't have a dream every night, that's okay. Just write down the next dream you have.

_____ / _____ / _____

_____

_____

_____

_____

_____

_____

_____

_____

_____

_____

_____

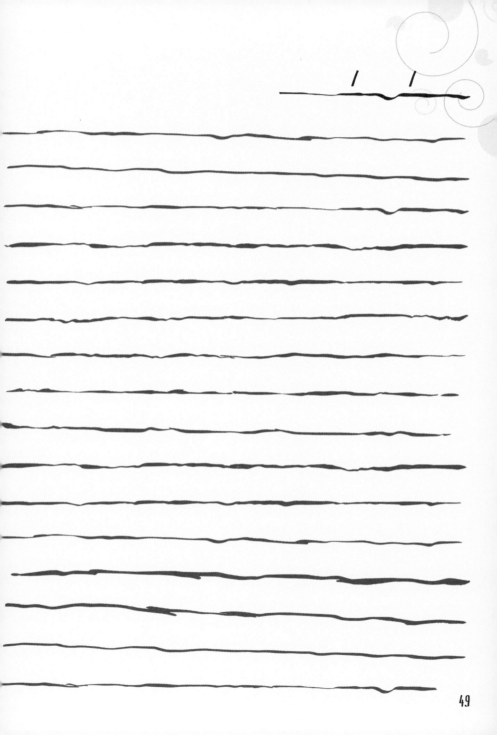

DREAM JARS

You can make your own dream jar at home!

YOU WILL NEED:

Empty clear soda bottle, any size, with lid

Cheap bottle of hair gel, in a size similar to your soda bottle

Water

Glitter

Glitter glue

Superglue

Any other small objects you'd like to see in your dream jar! If you can fit it in the bottle, you can make it part of the dream jar. Try using felt shapes or craft jewels. Or, for a fun twist, use GLOW-IN-THE-DARK paint.

HOW TO MAKE A DREAM JAR:

Ask a giant for help if you need it! Put some GLITTER GLUE, GLOW-IN-THE-DARK PAINT (if you're using any), and any GLITTER or other objects you're using into the SODA BOTTLE. Then squeeze in the bottle of HAIR GEL till the soda bottle is mostly full. Add water if the mixture is too thick. Then superglue the cap onto the bottle and you're done!

MIXING A DREAM

"It is a little bit like mixing a cake," the BFG said. "If you is putting the right amounts of all the different things into it, you is making the cake come out any way you want, sugary, splongy, curranty, Christmassy, or grobswitchy. It is the same with dreams."

"I see what you mean," Sophie said. "But I didn't know you could mix one dream with another."

"Dreams *like* being mixed," the BFG answered. "They is getting very lonesome all by themselves in those glassy bottles."

Take the best pieces from your dream journal and put them together to make a wonderful new golden PHIZZWIZARD!

54

Would your PHIZZWIZARD be a better dream for a boy, a girl, or both? Why?

_____

_____

_____

_____

_____

_____

Dreams are wonderful, especially the good dreams blown to children by the BFG.

But what about daydreams? Do you like night dreaming or daydreaming better?

_____

_____

_____

_____

What are your favorite things to daydream about?

_____

_____

_____

_____

_____

_____

_____

THE TROGGLEHUMPERS

Taking infinite care, the BFG unscrewed the top of the glass jar and tipped the squiggling squirming faintly scarlet trogglehumper into the wide end of his long trumpet. He put the other end of the trumpet to his lips. He aimed the instrument directly at the Fleshlumpeater's face. He took a deep breath, puffed out his cheeks, and then *whoof*! He blew!

What kind of things make for an upsetting dream? What would be in your worst TROGGLEHUMPER?

The BFG and Sophie need five more trogglehumpers to scare away the giants! Pick three scary ideas to create one trogglehumper for each giant. Write their names and the topics for their trogglehumper bad dreams.

GIANT'S NAME: _____

THREE SCARY IDEAS:

1. _____
2. _____
3. _____

GIANT'S NAME: _____

THREE SCARY IDEAS:

1. _____
2. _____
3. _____

GIANT'S NAME: _____

THREE SCARY IDEAS:

1. _____

2. _____

3. _____

GIANT'S NAME: _____

THREE SCARY IDEAS:

1. _____

2. _____

3. _____

GIANT'S NAME: _____

THREE SCARY IDEAS:

1. _____

2. _____

3. _____

HUMAN BEANS

59

The BFG has a special dream blower shaped like a trumpet. Here's how to make a special dream blower of your own:

YOU WILL NEED:

Empty water bottle

Duct tape or rubber band

Sock

Dish soap

Shallow empty container

Food coloring

HOW TO MAKE A DREAM BLOWER:

1. Cut off the bottom of the bottle.

2. Pull the sock over the bottom of your bottle and secure it with the duct tape or rubber band.

3. Pour a small amount of water, a few drops of dish soap, and a bit of food coloring into a shallow container and mix gently.

4. Dip the sock-covered end of the bottle into the mixture and blow through the top to create colorful dream bubbles!

Draw a picture of one of the scary dreams you created for the giants, or mix them up into one great trogglehumper and imagine what it might look like!

CAPTURING THE GIANTS

Sophie and the BFG have decided it's time to do something about the giants. The BFG wants to share his plan for catching the giants, but he's so excited, his ideas have come out all jumbled! Can you put them in order?

#___ AFTER THE DREAM, THE QUEEN WILL SEE SOPHIE ON HER WINDOWSILL.

#___ TIE UP THE GIANTS WITH ROPE WHILE THEY SLEEP.

#___ SOPHIE WILL EXPLAIN THAT WHAT HAPPENED IN THE QUEEN'S DREAM WAS REAL.

#___ CREEP UP ON THE GIANTS WHEN THEY ARE SLEEPING.

#___ MIX A DREAM TO DELIVER TO THE QUEEN OF ENGLAND.

#___ CARRY THE GIANTS BACK TO LONDON WITH THE HELICOPTERS.

#___ THE QUEEN WILL HELP CAPTURE THE GIANTS BY SENDING THE ARMY AND AIR FORCE WITH HELICOPTERS.

BEING A GOOD FRIEND

"But please understand that I cannot be helping it if I sometimes is saying things a little squiggly. I is trying my very best all the time." The Big Friendly Giant looked suddenly so forlorn that Sophie got quite upset.

"I'm sorry," she said. "I didn't mean to be rude."

Even though Sophie loves the BFG, she accidentally hurt his feelings.

Has a friend ever hurt your feelings? What did you do when that happened?

_____

_____

_____

_____

_____

_____

Have you ever hurt a friend's feelings?
How can you fix things when you
make a mistake?

_____

_____

_____

_____

_____

_____

_____

_____

What advice would you give to Sophie?

_____

_____

_____

_____

_____

_____

"I think you speak beautifully," Sophie said.

"You do?" cried the BFG, suddenly brightening. "You really do?"

"Simply beautifully," Sophie repeated.

When the BFG speaks, he uses lots of interesting SIMILES , or comparisons.

The BFG tells Sophie that his toes are as big as BUMPLEHAMMERS, and that human beans taste like STRAWBUNKLES and cream to other giants.

Can you complete the similes here?

SOPHIE IS AS BRAVE AS _____.

THE BFG IS AS TALL AS _____.

THE GIANTS ARE AS MEAN AS _____.

I AM AS EXCITED AS _____.

FROBSCOTTLE IS DELICIOUS LIKE _____.

_____ AS A BROKEN HELICOPTER.

_____ LIKE MOLDY PEACHES.

_____ AS A SQUIRREL.

_____ AS A CLOWN AT A PARTY.

_____ LIKE A BROOM AFTER SWEEPING.

Now write some similes of your own.
See how creative you can be!

_____

_____

_____

_____

Sometimes the BFG gets his words jumbled.
But what if he got his letters jumbled instead?

Can you unscramble the words below for him?

neuQe   _____

ihoSpe   _____

zwiripzadzh   _____

gBi lineFydr naGti _____

hoprzpizwep   _____

gpehuoltregrm   _____

lBtroteodobl   _____

eslpFtuarmehle   _____

zumbcrenosz   _____

E S B R M C A L

The BFG's words are really mixed-up now! See if you can find the words you just unjumbled!

V	D	W	K	G	E	P	Y	O	H	Y	G	K	G	V	T
Q	F	K	O	V	U	N	E	S	U	V	U	E	O	Q	N
E	T	L	Y	K	E	W	U	N	K	B	Q	H	V	G	A
G	R	I	E	E	H	K	I	O	A	V	P	S	Y	Q	I
K	O	Q	U	S	W	B	Y	Z	W	Y	Y	O	E	Y	G
W	G	Q	P	W	H	I	Z	Z	P	O	P	P	E	R	Y
E	G	V	K	A	O	L	P	C	Q	H	Q	H	G	I	L
V	L	G	Y	K	I	A	U	U	G	V	U	I	O	K	D
O	E	V	Y	D	K	W	B	M	I	K	W	E	Y	P	N
Y	H	E	V	Q	A	V	H	B	P	D	P	V	D	K	E
K	U	A	Y	O	E	Y	G	E	U	E	Q	I	V	K	I
W	M	Q	V	D	K	K	O	R	Q	E	A	Y	H	W	R
U	P	H	I	Z	Z	W	I	Z	A	R	D	T	E	Q	F
R	E	L	T	T	O	B	D	O	O	L	B	W	E	O	G
Y	R	W	K	I	E	I	Y	P	O	E	K	Y	D	R	I
V	Y	E	V	Q	W	V	H	E	Q	K	I	Q	V	E	B

READY TO RUN

The great yellow wasteland lay dim and milky in the moonlight as the Big Friendly Giant went galloping across it.

Sophie, still wearing only her nightie, was reclining comfortably in a crevice of the BFG's right ear. Nobody, she told herself, had ever traveled in greater comfort.

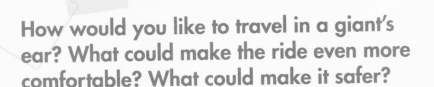

How would you like to travel in a giant's ear? What could make the ride even more comfortable? What could make it safer?

WELCOME TO LONDON

Sophie and the BFG go to London to give the Queen of England a dream.

Have you ever been to an entirely new place before? What did you do?

_____

_____

_____

_____

Do you like traveling to new places? Why or why not?

_____

_____

_____

_____

THE QUEEN

The Queen was still staring at Sophie. Gaping at her would be more accurate. Her mouth was slightly open, her eyes were round and wide as two saucers, and the whole of that famous rather lovely face was filled with disbelief.

Sophie meets the Queen of England under pretty strange circumstances! What would you say if you met the Queen?

When Sophie and the BFG have breakfast at the castle, Mr. Tibbs, the Queen's butler, makes sure that the meal goes without a hitch.

How much food do you think it would take to feed somebody as big as the BFG? What would you use for a table and chair?

Sophie and the BFG plan to trap all the giants, but it will be very dangerous. Fortunately, the BFG is very good at protecting Sophie. Do you ever protect your friends or family? How do you take care of them?

_____

_____

_____

_____

_____

_____

Who protects you and is the person who makes you feel most safe?

_____

_____

_____

_____

_____

_____

The Head of the Army and the Head of the Air Force think it would be better to get rid of all the giants rather than capture them.

What do you think about this plan? What punishment would you give the giants if you were in charge?

_____

_____

_____

_____

_____

_____

_____

_____

_____

Fortunately, the Queen prefers the BFG's plan. And it works!

The flushbunkled, gunzleswiped, bopmuggered giants are flown back to London as prisoners of Her Majesty.

What would you say to the captured giants if you could?

THE CELEBRATION

Every country in the world that had in the past been visited by the foul man-eating giants sent telegrams of congratulations and thanks to the BFG and to Sophie. Kings and Presidents and Prime Ministers and Rulers of every kind showered the enormous giant and the little girl with compliments and thankyous, as well as all sorts of medals and presents.

What is the nicest compliment you've ever given or received?

Sophie and the BFG go to live next to the Queen in the gardens of Windsor Great Park. The Queen has built a huge house for the BFG with a big bedroom and a special dream-sorting room.

What other rooms do you think are in the BFG's house? What does he keep there?

_____

_____

_____

_____

_____

The BFG and Sophie like to spend their afternoons outdoors in Windsor Great Park, reading and talking together. Where do you like to hang out with your friends?

_____

_____

_____

_____

_____

What do you like to do?
Describe your perfect day.

_____

_____

_____

_____

_____

_____

The BFG's old dream library from his cave can't compare to the wondrous new dream-sorting room in his new home! What do you think the BFG's new room looks like? How does he decorate it? What else does he keep in his dream room? Draw it here!

SNOZZCUMBERS

The Queen's Palace gardeners are growing SNOZZCUMBERS to feed to the giants, but the brilliant chefs at the palace have discovered a recipe that actually makes SNOZZCUMBERS taste SCRUMDIDDLYUMPTIOUS instead of sickable and maggotwise (though they're not going to tell the giants). Try the head chef's SNOZZCUMBER recipe at home!

YOU WILL NEED:

2 cucumbers (snozzcumbers), cut in half lengthwise

1/2 cup of your favorite kind of cream cheese

Any other small veggies you might like to add! Sophie recommends baby carrots or snow peas.

HOW TO MAKE SNOZZCUMBER BOATS:

1. Scoop or slice out some of the middle of the snozzcumber halves. Ask an adult to help you with this step.

2. Spoon the cream cheese into the snozzcumber shells.

3. Add veggies to the boats!

THE BFG DICTIONARY

The BFG would like your help putting some of his best words and their meanings into a dictionary. If you're not sure of a word's meaning, you can make up a definition based on how the word sounds.

SCRUMDIDDLYUMPTIOUS

_____
_____
_____
_____

BUNDONGLE

_____
_____
_____

UCKYSLUSH

_____
_____
_____
_____

WHOOSHEY

_____
_____
_____
_____

TELLY-TELLY BUNKUM BOX

_____

_____

_____

_____

WHIZZPOPPER

_____

_____

_____

_____

FLUNGAWAY

_____

_____

_____

SNOZZCUMBERS

_____

_____

_____

FROBSCOTTLE

_____

_____

_____

CHATBAGS

_____

_____

_____

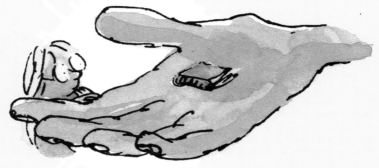

SLIMEWANGLER

_____

_____

_____

_____

_____

GROBSWITCHER

_____

_____

_____

_____

_____

JABBELING

_____

_____

_____

_____

BOGTHUMPER

_____

_____

_____

_____

PHIZZWIZARD

_____

_____

_____

_____

GOBBIT

_____

_____

_____

_____

ROMMYTOT

_____

_____

_____

_____

_____

SLUSHBUNGLE

_____

_____

_____

_____

_____

FLUSSED

_____

_____

_____

_____

_____

BELLYPOPPERS

_____

_____

_____

_____

"DON'T GOBBLEFUNK AROUND WITH WORDS"

Make up some words of your own and add them to the dictionary. If you need help, try combining some of the word pieces below!

SNOZZLE BUNK ZAMMER OPUS

FRAZ ZOP LAP NOP

GROG SLY JAMP RABBLE

_____   _____

_____   _____

_____   _____

_____   _____

_____   _____

The BFG would like to tell you about the first time he met the Queen. Can you help the BFG find the words to show he feels happy and nervous? Be as silly as you like!

Bounce my _____ ! Ginger my _____ !

I is feeling so _____ to be meeting

Her Majester. She is a most squackling lady.

I is never thunking for a titchy moment to be

_____ with human beans.

GIANTS

The rest of the giants are now held prisoner in a large pit. Do you think it is a good idea to keep them locked up in a pit? Why are some giants so rotsome, but the BFG is big and friendly?

_____

_____

_____

Would you go to the pit to speak to them? What would you say?

_____

_____

_____

Deep in the pit, the giants are talking about their old favorite human meals!

Humans from Wales taste of fish (even though whales aren't fish). Humans from Jersey taste like sweaters, and Turks from Turkey taste like turkey, of course. What do you think these humans taste like?

FINNS FROM FINLAND TASTE _____

RUSSIANS FROM RUSSIA TASTE _____

SWEDES FROM SWEDEN TASTE _____

ESTONIANS FROM ESTONIA TASTE _____

AUSTRIANS FROM AUSTRIA TASTE _____

CHILEANS FROM CHILE TASTE _____

THAIS FROM THAILAND TASTE _____

How do you think the
giants feel about being
captured? Do they think
it's fair or unfair? Why?

How do you feel when you are punished?

EXTRA! EXTRA!

Imagine that the Queen asked you to write a newspaper story about the BFG's adventures and how he and Sophie saved England from man-eating giants.

First, list all the characters:

_____

_____

_____

_____

Now write the headline for your story:

_____

Now write your article! Make it very interesting. Be sure to give background information about all the main characters, and include the emotions everyone felt. Pretend that you interviewed people, and include quotes from your interviews!

_____

_____

_____

_____

_____

_____

_____

_____

_____

_____

_____

_____

The BFG always dreamed of having an elephant for a pet! Perhaps now that he lives in Windsor Great Park, he will have enough room. If you could have any animal as a pet, what kind would you pick and why?

_____

_____

_____

_____

The BFG dreams of riding his elephant to pick peaches from the trees! What would you and your pet do together?

_____

_____

_____

_____

_____

Draw a picture of your animal and give him or her a name!

Imagine that the Queen let you build yourself a new home in Windsor Great Park, right next to the BFG's and Sophie's houses. You get to design it yourself. How many rooms will it have? What will they be?

Draw your new house so you can show the Queen exactly what you want!

The BFG wrote a whole book about his adventures with Sophie, the Queen, and the nine vicious giants. Maybe you've heard of this book!

What are some of the best books you've read?

What do you like best about your favorite book?

_____

_____

_____

_____

_____

_____

If you wrote a book about your own life, what would you call it? Draw a cover and include an exciting title in the space below.

Of all the places Sophie went with the BFG—
London, Giant Country, the BFG's cave, and
Dream Country—which is your favorite? Why?
What would you like to do there?

Sophie's life is much happier now that she lives with the BFG in Windsor Great Park.

Write a journal entry from Sophie's point of view, describing how she feels and what she thinks of all the adventures she's had.

Write a letter to Sophie and the BFG! Tell them about your life, ask them lots of questions, and be sure to thank them for keeping us all safe from bloodthirsty giants!

ANSWERS

1. Mix a dream...
2. After the dream...
3. Sophie will explain...
4. The Queen will help...
5. Creep up on...
6. Tie up the giants...
7. Carry the giants back...

Queen
Sophie
phizzwizard
Big Friendly Giant
whizzpopper
trogglehumper
Bloodbottler
Fleshlumpeater
snozzcumber

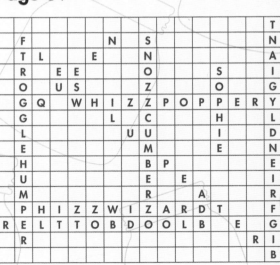

																T
	F					N		S								N
	T	L			E			N								A
	R	E	E					O					S			I
	O	U	S					Z					O			G
	G	Q		W	H	I	Z	Z	P	O	P	P	E	R		Y
	G				L			C					H			L
	L			U		U		M					I			D
	E					M		E					E			N
	H					B	P									E
	U					E		E								I
	M					R				A						R
	P	H	I	Z	Z	W	I	Z	A	R	D	T				F
R	E	L	T	T	O	B	D	O	O	L	B		E			G
	R													R		I
																B